At Home on the Mountain

Sharon Gordon

Marshall Cavendish
Benchmark
New York

This road goes up to my home.

It is on a mountain.

ABINGTON PUBLIC LIBRARY
3 1627 01037 8704

My house is strong.

It is safe in wind and storms.

Mountain weather can change quickly.

Getting home is not always easy.

Sometimes the road is muddy.

Sometimes it is covered with snow.

Our car can go over
rocks and ice.

Big tires keep it from
slipping.

Many animals *graze* near our home.

You never know when a bear will visit!

The air is cold on top of the mountain.

Eagles fly over the treetops.

We watch out for falling rocks.

Sliding snow can turn into an *avalanche*.

In spring, visitors fish in the streams.

They like the fresh mountain air.

In winter, they come to ski.

Workers on *snowmobiles* help them stay safe.

YAMAHA

We like to hike on the trails.

We wear backpacks and boots.

APPALACHIAN

On clear days, we can
see a long way.

On other days, our house
is in the clouds.

Our mountain home is exciting.

We can snowboard in our own backyard!

Mountain Home

bear

eagle

rocks

snowmobile

streams

trails

Challenge Words

avalanche (AV-uh-lanch) Heavy snow, ice, and rocks sliding quickly down a mountain.

graze (GRAYZ) To eat grass or other plants in a field.

snowmobiles (SNOW-moh-beels) Small vehicles that can be driven on the snow.

Index

Page numbers in **boldface** are illustrations.

About the Author

Sharon Gordon has written many books for young children. She has always worked as an editor. Sharon and her husband Bruce have three children, Douglas, Katie, and Laura, and one spoiled pooch, Samantha. They live in Midland Park, New Jersey.

With thanks to Nanci Vargus, Ed.D. and
Beth Walker Gambro, reading consultants

Marshall Cavendish Benchmark
Marshall Cavendish
99 White Plains Road
Tarrytown, New York 10591-9001
www.marshallcavendish.us

Gordon, Sharon.
At home on the mountain / by Sharon Gordon.
p. cm. — (Bookworms: at home)
Summary: "Describes life on a mountain, including avalanches
and snowmobiles"—Provided by publisher.
Includes index.
ISBN 0-7614-1961-6
1. Mountains—Juvenile literature. I. Title. II. Series: Gordon, Sharon.
Bookworms. At home.
QH87.G67 2005
551.43'2—dc22
2004025385

Photo Research by Anne Burns Images

Cover Photo by *Corbis*/John M. Roberts

The photographs in this book are used with permission and through the courtesy of:
Corbis: p. 1 James Randklev; p. 3 Darwin Wiggett; p. 5 Joseph Sohm/Visions of America;
pp. 7, 17, 27, 28 (lower l.) Royalty Free; pp. 13, 28 (upper l.) Stan Osolinski;
pp. 15, 28 (upper r.) Ron Sanford; pp. 19, 29 (left) Mark E. Gibson; pp. 21, 28 (lower r.) David
Stoecklein; pp. 23, 29 (right) John Henley; p. 25 James Randklev. *Woodfin Camp*: p. 9 Sepp Seitz.
Index Stock Imagery: p. 11 Stewart Cohen.

Series design by Becky Terhune

Printed in Malaysia
1 3 5 6 4 2

Children's Songs and Fingerplays

By
Pamela Conn Beall and
Susan Hagen Nipp

Illustrated by
Nancy Spence Klein

Wiggleworm workout

LOOBY LOO

2. left hand
   (After each verse, join hands and circle around on chorus.)
3. right foot
4. left foot
5. head
6. whole self

Actions:
a) join hands, circle to left   b) stop circling, do as words indicate throughout verse

NOW TALL, NOW SMALL

Actions:
a) squatting position to standing b) back to squatting c) curl into a ball

ANIMAL POEM
(Action Poem)

Pam Beall

I'm a little kitty,
 I love to tippy toe.
Won't you do it with me?
 Ready now, let's go.

I'm a little rabbit,
 I love to hop, hop, hop.
Come on and do it with me.
 It's fun; we'll never stop

I'm a great big elephant,
 I take big steps so slow.
I'd love to have you join me,
 Ready now? Let's go.

I'm a little dog,
 I love to run and run.
If you would do it with me,
 We could have such fun.

WALKING, WALKING

(Tune: Are You Sleeping? p. 15)

Walking, walking, walking, walking,
Hop, hop, hop, hop, hop, hop.

Running, running, running,
Running, running, running,

Now let's stop, now let's stop.

JIMMY CRACK CORN

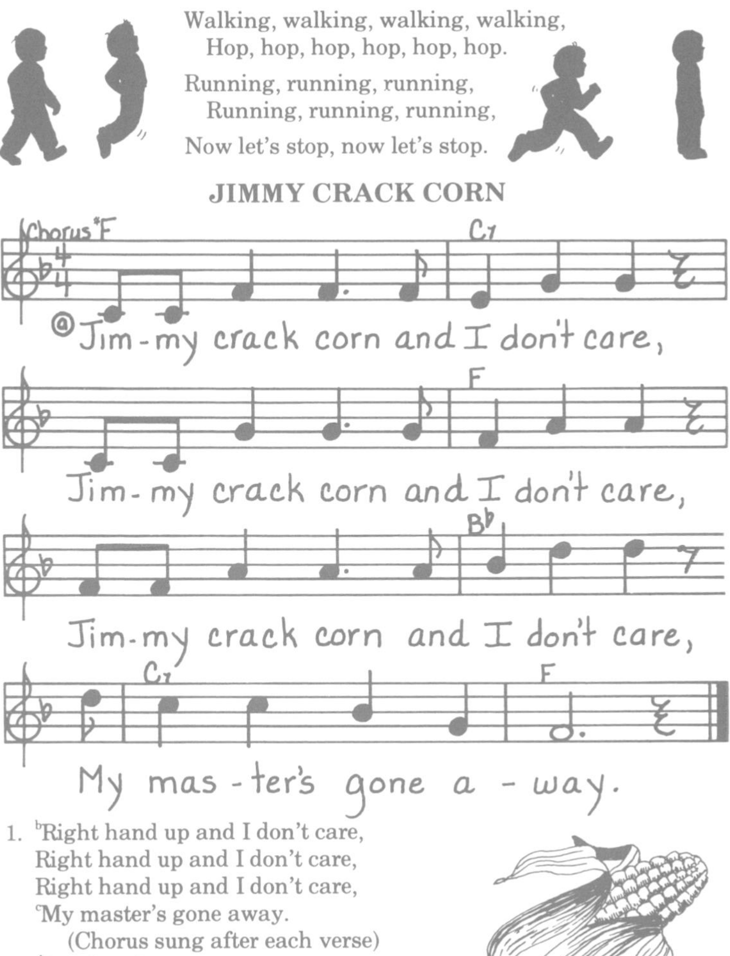

1. [b]Right hand up and I don't care,
   Right hand up and I don't care,
   Right hand up and I don't care,
   [c]My master's gone away.
   (Chorus sung after each verse)
2. [d]Left hand up...
3. [e]Both hands up...

Actions:
a) circle to left throughout chorus b) hold right hand up and walk to center of circle
c) hand down, move back out to form circle d) hold left hand up, walk to center of circle e) both hands up, walk to center of circle

* Guitar play in E (E, A, B7)

Actions:
a) on arms and knees, fetal position, head down b) head pops up c) tail pops up
d) stand up e) flap elbows f) flap arms g) twirl around and around h) fall down

RING AROUND THE ROSY

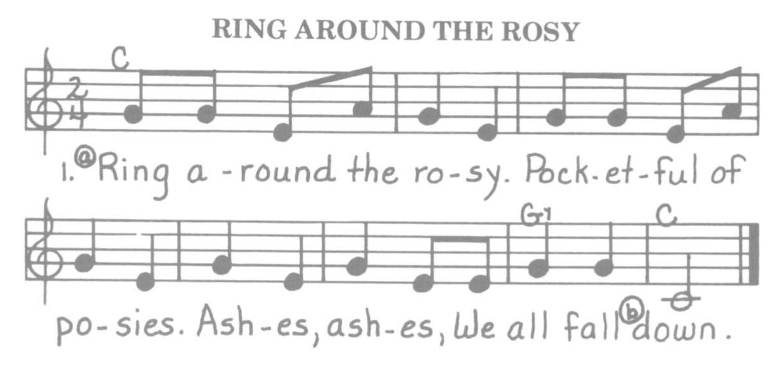

2. Tiptoe 'round the rosy...
3. Skip
4. Hop
5. Run

Actions:
a) join hands, circle to left
b) all fall down

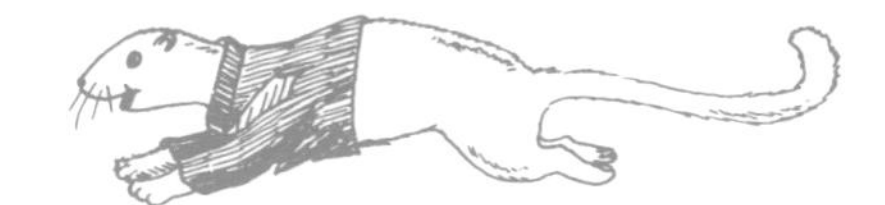

POP! GOES THE WEASEL

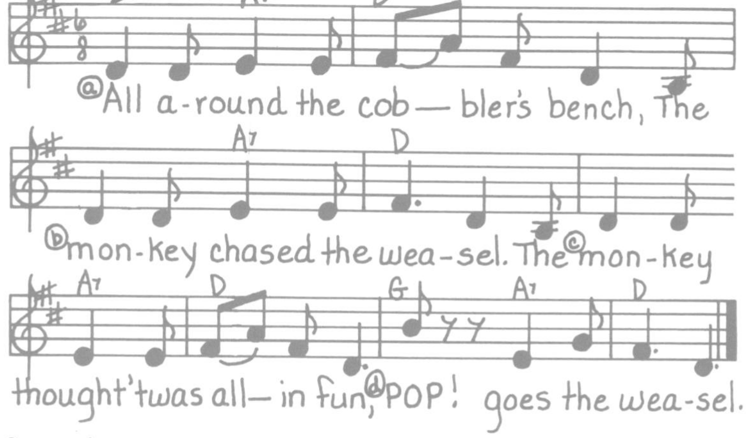

Suggestions:

1. Roll hands while singing, clap on POP.
2. Walk in circle, fall on POP.

Actions:
a) make circle in air with finger b) chase one hand with the other hand c) hands at either side of head, rock sideways d) clap

ONE FINGER, ONE THUMB

2. One finger, one thumb, one hand keep moving....
3. ....two hands....
4. ....one arm....
5. ....two arms....
6. ....one leg....
7. ....two legs....
8. ....sit down, stand up....

Actions: Move parts of the body as song indicates.

THE MULBERRY BUSH

1. This is the way we wash our face
2. Comb our hair
3. Brush our teeth
4. Put on our clothes
5. Etc.

Suggestion: For circle game, join hands and circle around on chorus after each verse. Act out motions on verses.

IF YOU'RE HAPPY

2. . . . stomp your feet (stomp, stomp) . . .
3. . . . shout hurray (Hurray!) . . .
4. . . . do all three (clap, clap, stomp, stomp, hurray!) . . .

* Guitar play in E (E, A, B7)

PETER HAMMERS

(Tune: What Are You Wearing? p. 28)

1. Peter hammers with one hammer, one hammer,
   one hammer, (pound one fist on floor or leg)
   Peter hammers with one hammer all day long.
2. Two hammers (pound two fists)
3. Three hammers (pound two fists, one foot)
4. Four hammers (pound two fists, two feet)
5. Five hammers (pound two fists, two feet, nod head up and down)
6. Peter's very tired now... (rub eyes, then lay head on hands)

REACH FOR THE SKY

THREE BLUE PIGEONS

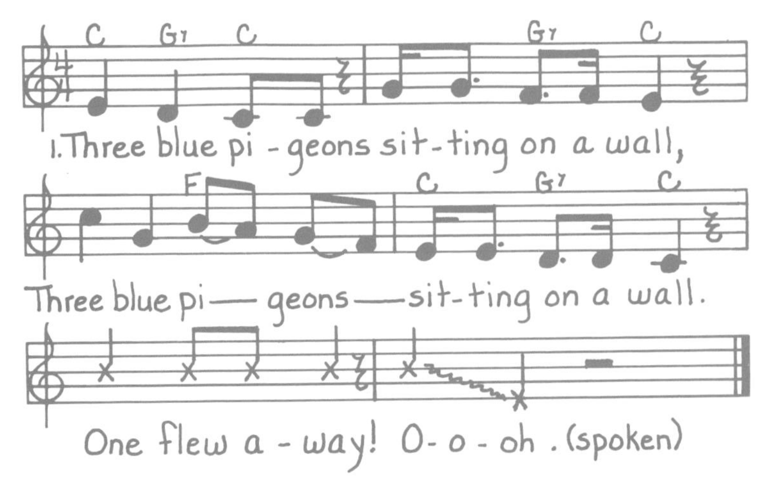

2. Two blue pigeons sitting on a wall,
   Two blue pigeons sitting on a wall.
   Another flew away! O-o-o-o-o-h. (spoken)
3. One blue pigeon sitting on a wall,
   One blue pigeon sitting on a wall.
   And the third flew away! O-o-o-o-o-h.
4. No blue pigeons sitting on a wall,
   No blue pigeons sitting on a wall.
   One flew back! Whee-ee-ee-ee!
5. One blue pigeon sitting on a wall,
   One blue pigeon sitting on a wall.
   Another flew back! Whee-ee-ee-ee!
6. Two blue pigeons sitting on a wall,
   Two blue pigeons sitting on a wall.
   And the third flew back! Whee-ee-ee-ee!
7. Three blue pigeons sitting on a wall,
   Three blue pigeons sitting on a wall.
   (Clap happily while singing)

Suggestion: Three children sit on a bench. All children sing while the three act out the words.

ONE ELEPHANT WENT OUT TO PLAY

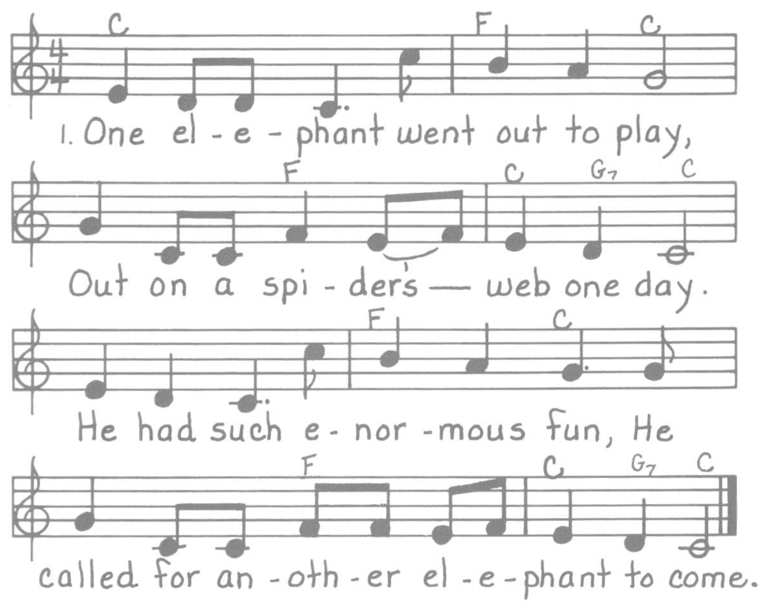

2. Two elephants went out to play . . .
3. Three elephants went out to play, etc.

Game: One child walks around room like an elephant. At the end of the verse, he chooses another 'elephant' to join behind him. At the end of each verse, the last 'elephant' chosen selects a new 'elephant'. Continue until several children are imitating elephants.

HEAD AND SHOULDERS

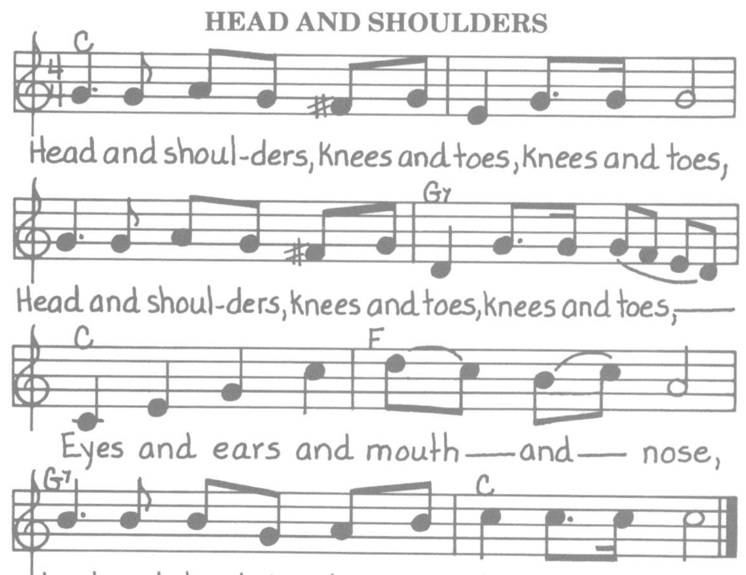

Suggestions: Point to body parts as singing. Repeat, leaving out different body parts each time.

JACK AND JILL

(Scale Song)

Actions:

a) squat down and as notes move up, move body slowly to standing position b) start moving down as notes move down ending in squatting position

THIS IS THE WAY

(Tune: Mulberry Bush, p. 41)

1. This is the way the ladies ride,
   Ladies ride, ladies ride,
   This is the way the ladies ride,
   Tri-tree, tri-tree, tri-tree.
   (bounce child gently on knees)
2. Gentlemen ride — gallop-a-gallop-a-trot!
   (bounce faster)
3. Farmers ride — hobbledy-hobbledy-hoy!
   (bounce harder)

TROT TO BOSTON

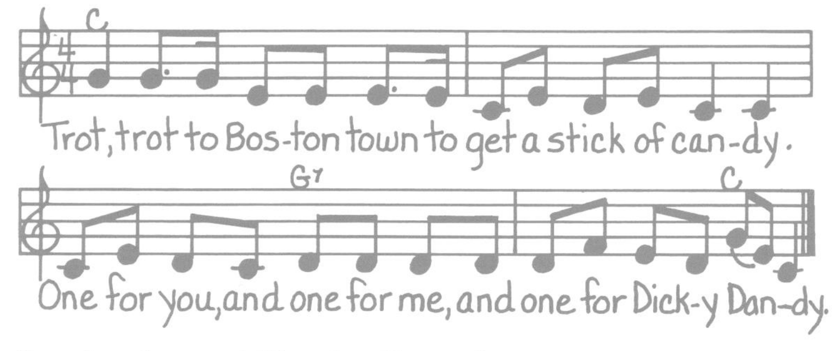

Cross legs, bounce child on foot. Near end of song, gently drop child to floor (surprise).

2. Teddy Bear, Teddy Bear, go upstairs,
   Teddy Bear, Teddy Bear, say your prayers,
Teddy Bear, Teddy Bear, switch off the light,
   Teddy Bear, Teddy Bear, say good-night.

Pantomime the words.

Whew! It's bedtime.

Suggestion: Substitute child's name for 'baby.'

* Guitar play in E (E, A, B7)

SLEEP, BABY, SLEEP

F C7 F C7 F

Sleep, ba-by, sleep. Your fa-ther tends the sheep.

C7 F

Your moth-er shakes the dream-land tree, Down

C7 F C7 F

falls a lit-tle dream for thee. Sleep, ba-by, sleep.

ALL NIGHT, ALL DAY

1. When at night I go to sleep,
   Angels watchin' over me, my Lord,
   Pray the Lord my soul to keep,
   Angels watchin' over me.

   (Repeat chorus)

* Guitar play in E (E, A, B7)

ALL THE PRETTY LITTLE HORSES
Dm
Gm
Am
Hush-a-bye, don't you cry, Go to sleep-y lit-tle
When you wake, you shall have all the pret-ty lit-tle
Dm
Am
Dm
ba-by. Blacks and bays, dap-ples and grays,
hors-es.
Am
Dm
coach and six-a-lit-tle hors-es. Hush-a-bye,
Gm
Am
Dm
don't you cry, Go to sleep-y lit-tle ba-by.

HUSH, LITTLE BABY

2. If that mockingbird don't sing,
   Papa's gonna buy you a diamond ring.
3. If that diamond ring turns brass,
   Papa's gonna buy you a looking glass.
4. If that looking glass gets broke,
   Papa's gonna buy you a billy goat.
5. If that billy goat don't pull,
   Papa's gonna buy you a cart and bull.
6. If that cart and bull turn over,
   Papa's gonna buy you a dog named Rover.
7. If that dog named Rover don't bark,
   Papa's gonna buy you a horse and cart.
8. If that horse and cart fall down,
   You'll still be the sweetest little baby in town.

Another holiday . . . so soon?
Be Mine

JACK-O-LANTERN
(Fingerplay)

Sometimes big and sometimes small,
(arms form large circle, then small)

But always round and yellow,
(draw circle in air)

When children make my famous grin,
(grin, showing teeth)

Then I'm a scary fellow.
(make scary face)

CHICKAMY, CHICKAMY, CRANEY CROW

Game: Choose a child to be the witch. The witch hides her eyes and turns her back while a group of children sing in a teasing way near her. At the count of twelve, the witch comes out of hiding and tries to catch as many children as she can. Children are 'safe' if they reach a predetermined point.

TEN LITTLE WITCHES

(Tune: Ten Little Indians, p. 31)

1. One little, two little, three little witches,
   Four little, five little, six little witches,
   Seven little, eight little, nine little witches,
   Ten witches in the sky.
2. Ten little, nine little, eight little witches,
   Seven little, six little, five little witches,
   Four little, three little, two little witches,
   One little witch, "Bye, bye!"

GOBBLE, GOBBLE

(Fingerplay)

[a]A turkey is a funny bird,
[b]His head goes wobble, wobble,
And he knows [c]just one word,
[d]Gobble, gobble, gobble.

Actions:
a) make turkey tail by hooking thumbs and spreading fingers b) shake from side to side c) hold up one finger d) shake head, sound like turkey

OVER THE RIVER

2. Over the river and through the woods,
   Trot fast my dapple gray.
   Spring over the ground like a hunting hound
   For this is Thanksgiving Day.
   Over the river and through the woods,
   Now Grandmother's face I spy.
   Hurrah for the fun, is the pudding done?
   Hurrah for the pumpkin pie.

CHRISTMAS IS COMING

S. Nesbitt 1600's

Suggestion: Can be sung as a round

THE CHIMNEY
(Fingerplay)

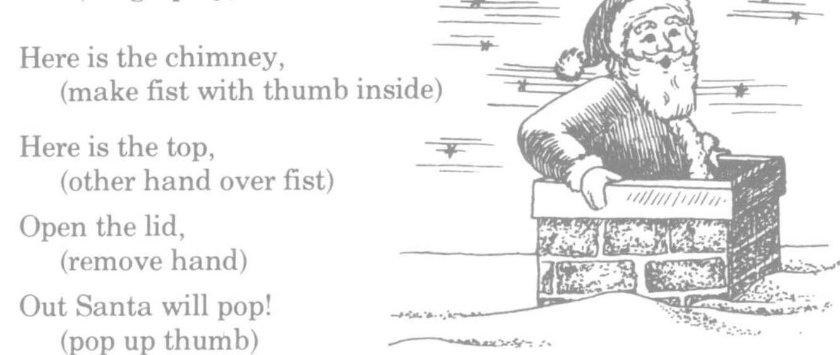

Here is the chimney,
(make fist with thumb inside)

Here is the top,
(other hand over fist)

Open the lid,
(remove hand)

Out Santa will pop!
(pop up thumb)

WE WISH YOU A MERRY CHRISTMAS

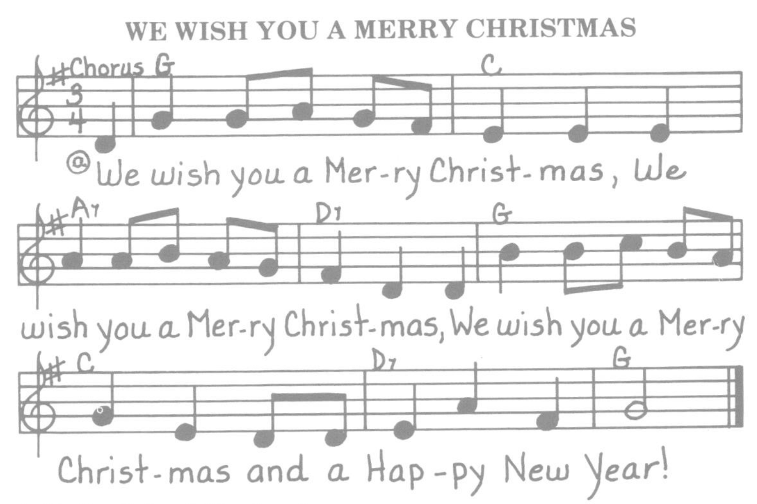

1. [b]Let's all do a little clapping,
   Let's all do a little clapping,
   Let's all do a little clapping,
   And spread Christmas cheer.

   (Chorus sung after each verse)

2. [c]Jumping
3. [d]Twirling

Suggestion: Add your own verses.

Actions:
a) join hands, circle to left, continuing throughout chorus b) clap hands c) jump in place d) twirl in place

SKIDAMARINK

Actions:
a) right elbow in left hand, wiggle fingers b) left elbow in right hand, wiggle fingers c) point to self d) hug self e) point to other person f) arms form circle above head, lean left g) keep circle above head, stand straight h) keep circle above head, lean right i) sweep arms down and form new circle above head